For Florence and Benicia

Text copyright © Judy Taylor 1983.
Illustrations copyright © Susan Gantner 1983.
All rights reserved. First published in the
United States of American 1984 by Philomel Books,
a division of The Putnam Publishing Group, New York.
Printed in England.
First published in Great Britain by The Bodley Head, London.

Library of Congress Cataloging in Publication Data

Taylor, Judy 1932 –
Sophie and Jack Help Out.

Summary: There are lots of surprises in store
when two young hippos do the spring planting in
the vegetable garden.
[1. Vegetable gardening – Fiction. 2. Gardening –
Fiction. 3. Hippopotamus – Fiction.] I. Gantner,
Susan, ill.
II. Title.
PZ7.T21476 Sop 1984   [E]   83-13302
ISBN 0-399-21059-8

Sophie and Jack Help Out

JUDY TAYLOR

Illustrated by Susan Gantner

PHILOMEL BOOKS
New York

Spring had arrived.

But everyone was worried.

Papa could not plant the vegetables.

He was not well.

"I'll do it," said Sophie.

"I'll help," said Jack.

So they dug

and they weeded,

they raked

and they planted.

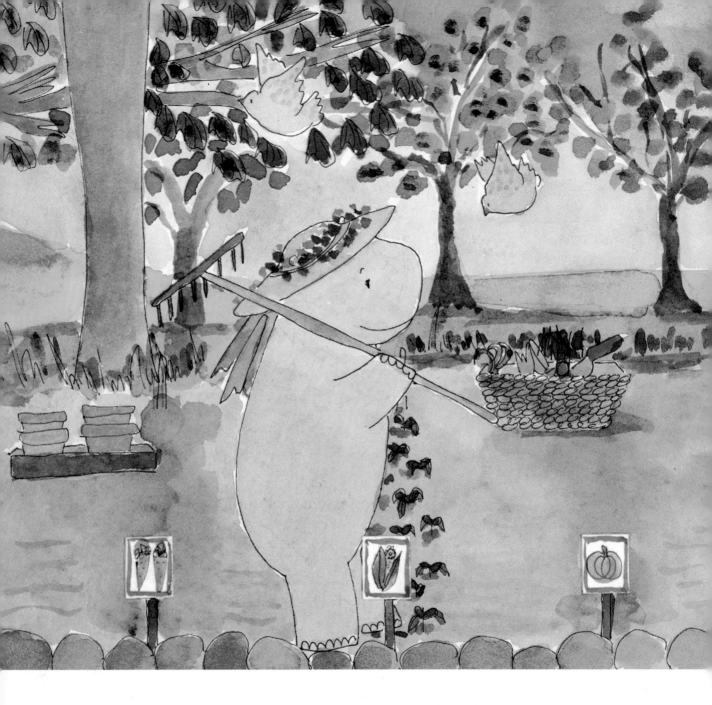

Soon it was all done.

But that night the wind roared

and the rain poured.

The garden was a mess.

"I'll fix it," said Jack.

"I'll help," said Sophie.

When the vegetables were ready

there were many surprises.

Can you see why?